QUIET WYATT

TAMMI SAUER

ILLUSTRATED BY ARTHUR HOWARD

CLARION BOOKS
Houghton Mifflin Harcourt
Boston   New York

Clarion Books
3 Park Avenue
New York, New York 10016

Text copyright © 2018 by Tammi Sauer
Illustrations copyright © 2018 by Arthur Howard

Clarion Books is an imprint of
Houghton Mifflin Harcourt Publishing Company.

hmhco.com

The illustrations in this book were done in watercolor, gouache, and pencil.
The text type was set in humper.

Library of Congress Cataloging-in-Publication Data
Names: Sauer, Tammi, author. | Howard, Arthur, illustrator. Title: Quiet Wyatt / by Tammi Sauer ;
illustrated by Arthur Howard. Description: Boston ; New York : Houghton Mifflin Harcourt, [2018] |
Summary: A friendship is born when soft-spoken Wyatt is paired with outgoing Noreen on a class field
trip.Identifiers: LCCN 2017015653 | ISBN 9780544113305 Subjects: | CYAC: Friendship--Fiction. |
School field trips--Fiction. Classification: LCC PZ7.S2502 Qu 2018 | DDC [E]--dc23

Manufactured in China
SCP 10 9 8 7 6 5 4 3 2 1
4500713576

For quiet kids, noisy kids, and every kid in between

—T.S.

Wyatt liked quiet.
And being quiet worked for Wyatt.

He was a spectacular tree
in the school play.

He was the model visitor
at the dinosaur museum.

He was a total star at ninja camp.

Wyatt's world was
perfectly quiet . . .

. . . until his class went on a field trip
and he was paired with Noreen.
Noreen was anything but quiet.

"I'm the *queen* of nature," said Noreen.
"Let's do this, field trip buddy!"
Wyatt gulped. Quietly, of course.

"Fishing is my specialty," said Noreen.
"This is how to cast a line."

Wyatt gaped. Quietly, of course.

"I was born for boating," said Noreen.
"This is how to paddle a canoe."

Wyatt dripped. Quietly, of course.

"Wow," said Noreen. "I'm so good at noticing the details, it's scary."

It was a very busy field trip.

There was bird-watching.
"Binoculars are for beginners, Wyatt."

There was hiking.

"This is what you call trailblazing, Wyatt."

There was ziplining.
"Don't look down, Wyatt!"

Somebody got *extra* quiet.

When it was time to return to the bus,
Noreen had lots to say.
"Nature's not *all* I'm good at.
There's math and cartwheels and . . .
Oops! Almost forgot.
I have the gift of song."

One thing was clear.
For the first time in the history of Wyatt,
he could not stay quiet.

La La
La La
La La

"NOREEN! ROCKS!"

"Thanks," said Noreen.
"Glad you think so!"

Then . . .

"Uh-oh," said Noreen.

Scoop.

Everyone was wowed.

Especially Noreen.

"I'm an excellent ninja," said Wyatt.

"Good to know, field trip buddy," said Noreen.

The bus headed back to school.
"Hey, Mr. Driver," said Noreen.
"I know a shortcut!"

Wyatt didn't know *what* to say.
So he stayed quiet.

But, from time to time,
Wyatt wasn't so quiet.

"See?" said Wyatt.

"*Oh*," said Noreen.
Wyatt smiled. Quietly, of course.
He still liked quiet.

He also liked having a friend.